Sometimes I'm a... MONSTER!

Gillian Shields * Georgie Birkett

PICTURE CORGI

Sometimes I'm an *angel* -
helpful, sweet and kind . . .

and sometimes I'm a MONSTER,
with mischief on my mind!

Angels tidy up
their toys . . .

but MONSTERS just don't care. We get them out and make a mess,

and leave them EVERYWHERE.

Now all the little MONSTERS
are coming out to play.
We make the grown-ups rather cross -

we WON'T do
what they say.

MONSTERS snatch
and **push**
and **shove,**

MONSTERS know
wild games...

That soon turn into quarrels,

when we call each other names.

But *angels* share so nicely,

and wait to have a turn . . .

They're kind
to friends

and love
their pets . . .

they like to sit and learn.

Angels help to serve the tea,
and hand around the cake.

They always say, "Please may I?"
They never grab and take.

We MONSTERS splash at bath time,
and spill our bedtime drink.

"Do be careful!" Mummy says.
MONSTERS just don't think!

But when it's time
to go to bed

and dream
about the day,

I'm sorry for
the times

I've been a MONSTER
in my way . . .

And I promise that tomorrow,
when the day is fresh and new,

I'll be the little *angel*
who is loved so
much by you!

For Jayden Sherwood and his brothers – G.S.

For Caz, Nick & Olive – G.B.

SOMETIMES I'M A MONSTER
A PICTURE CORGI BOOK 978 0 552 57606 2
Published in Great Britain by Picture Corgi
an imprint of Random House Children's Publishers UK
A Random House Group Company
This edition published 2013

3 5 7 9 10 8 6 4 2

Text copyright © Gillian Shields, 2013
Illustrations copyright © Georgie Birkett, 2013
The right of Gillian Shields and Georgie Birkett to be identified as the author and illustrator
of this work has been asserted in accordance with the Copyright, Designs and Patents Act 1988.

Picture Corgi Books are published by Random House Children's Publishers UK,
61–63 Uxbridge Road, London W5 5SA
www.**randomhousechildrens**.co.uk

www.**randomhouse**.co.uk

Addresses for companies within The Random House Group Limited can be found at: www.randomhouse.co.uk/offices.htm
THE RANDOM HOUSE GROUP Limited Reg. No. 954009
A CIP catalogue record for this book is available from the British Library.
Printed in China